THIS BOOK BELONGS TO

____

ISBN 9798377887461

PUBLISHED BY PASTEL PUBLISHING, 2023

BEARLY'S BEACH-DAY ADVENTURE

BY RANYA-ARMANI (AND MOM)

HI, I'M BEARLY

BEARLY LOVES THE BEACH,
BEARLY LOVES THE SUN,
BEARLY LOVES TO RELAX ON
THE SAND AND HAVE FUN...

THE SAND IS SO WARM,
HMMM...

THE SEA IS SPARKLY BLUE,
THE SEA CREATURES
SCURRY UP AND DOWN,
AND THE SAND IS LIKE A WARM
BLANKET ON THE GROUND...
LET'S GO
PLAY!

z z Z Z Z

BEARLY RELAXES IN THE SUN,
AND ENJOYS THE SEA BREEZE,
OH, WHAT A WONDERFUL DAY
TO NAP UNDER THE
PALM TREES...

THAT NAP MADE ME HUNGRY...

BEARLY PACKS A PICNIC,
SOME DELICIOUS
HOME-MADE TREATS,
WHO DOESN'T LOVE MOUTH-
WATERING SWEETS...?

BEARLY GOES FOR A SWIM,
WHAT A SPLENDID WAY
TO COOL DOWN,
BEARLY WISHES THERE WAS
A SEA BACK HOME, IN TOWN...

HMMM...
THIS IS REFRESHING

BEARLY EATS A POPSICLE,
A DELIGHTFUL FROZEN SNACK,
AS THE SUN WARMS UP
BEARLY'S FURRY BACK...

MMM...
CHERRY FLAVOUR...

BEARLY LOOKS FOR SEA SHELLS,
AND SCAVENGES FOR THE
PRETTIEST OF THEM ALL,
ALL SO UNIQUE, SOME QUITE BIG
AND SOME REALLY SMALL...

THIS IS MY FAVOURITE SHELL...

I LOVE YOU FISH...
CAN I GET A HUG TOO...?

BEARLY GOES FISHING,
IT'S SUCH A RELAXING SPORT,
BUT BEARLY ONLY FISHES
FOR FUN AND RELEASES
WHAT IS CAUGHT...

BEARLY DECIDES TO GO SURFING,
AND CATCHES WAVE AFTER
WAVE LIKE A PRO,
"LOOK AT ME BALANCING,
SURFS UP BRO..."

THIS IS SO MUCH FUN!
CAN I HAVE A GO?

BEARLY FLYS A KITE,
THE WIND CARRIES IT UP HIGH
IN THE BRIGHT BLUE SKY,
IT'S EVEN HIGHER THAN THE
BIRDS FLYING BY...

I LOVE MY PURPLE KITE...

BEARLY BUILDS SAND-CASTLES,
IT'S ONE OF BEARLY'S
FAVOURITE THINGS TO DO,
"OH MY, LOOK AT THE TIME,
IT TOTALLY JUST FLEW..."

THIS IS THE BEST
SAND-CASTLE EVER...!

BEARLY PACKS UP FOR THE DAY, IT'S TIME TO HEAD BACK HOME, "THANKS FOR COMING TO THE BEACH WITH ME, I CAN'T WAIT TO ENJOY A BUBBLE BATH, FILLED TO THE BRIM WITH FOAM..."

THE END

www.ingramcontent.com/pod-product-compliance
Lightning Source LLC
LaVergne TN
LVHW071231160826
845679LV00003B/957

* 9 7 9 8 3 7 7 8 8 7 4 6 1 *